THE INFAMOUS RATSOS

Camp Out

THE INFAMOUS RATSOS

Camp Out

Kara LaReau

illustrated by Matt Myers

CANDLEWICK PRESS

Text copyright © 2020 by Kara LaReau
Illustrations copyright © 2020 by Matt Myers

First paperback edition 2021

Library of Congress Catalog Card Number 2020904990
ISBN 978-1-5362-0006-5 (hardcover)
ISBN 978-1-5362-1903-6 (paperback)

21 22 23 24 25 26 TRC 10 9 8 7 6 5 4 3 2 1

Printed in Eagan, MN, USA

This book was typeset in Scala.
The illustrations were done in ink and watercolor dye on paper.

Candlewick Press
99 Dover Street
Somerville, Massachusetts 02144

www.candlewick.com

To my fellow Velma Diggses
K. L.

For Glenn Trussell, who is more likely
to smile in the woods than at a party
M. M.

STREETS AND AVENUES

The Infamous Ratsos are leaving the Big City . . . temporarily.

"We're almost there, Big City Scouts!" says Big Lou.

"All our Scout meetings and activities in the city have been fun, but it's going to be nice to get away for a while," says Ralphie. "I've never even been camping, and I know I'm going to love it."

"I'm going to love all the badges I'm going to earn on this trip," says Louie, admiring his vest. "We've only been Scouts for a few months, and I already have Organizing, Leadership, City Smarts, Cleanup, and Good Neighbor, not to mention my Avenue pin."

"I wish I wasn't just a Street," Ralphie says. "It's going to take forever for me to be old enough to be an Avenue, like you and Sid and Kurt."

"I think I just saw a sign for the Friendly Woods Campground!" says Millicent.

"Exactly the distance I predicted," says Velma Diggs, consulting her calculator.

"I can't believe she brought a *calculator* on a *camping trip*," says Kurt Musky. "Typical little Street."

"Typical *nerd*," says Sid Chitterer.

"Actually, I think it's cool that Velma's into numbers," Ralphie informs them. "I'm terrible at math."

"I wish Fluffy had come with us, and Chad," Tiny says with a sigh.

"I even brought bags of Happy Puffs for him, since I know how he loves his snacks," says Ralphie.

"Fluffy said something about a 'rutabaga emergency' in her garden," Millicent reminds him. "And Chad has allergies."

"Well, he's missing out," Ralphie says.

"We're missing out, too. This trip won't be the same without them," says Tiny.

"That's the truth," says Millicent. "Though I think Velma has potential."

"Here we are!" says Big Lou, steering the van into the parking lot.

"Wait. That truck next to us looks familiar," says Louie.

"The guy next to the truck looks *really* familiar," says Ralphie.

"Greetings, Big City Scouts!" says
Grandpa Ratso.

"Grandpa!" say the Ratso brothers.

"Grandpa was my Big City Scoutmaster when I was your age," Big Lou explains. "He's here to show you all the ropes."

Grandpa Ratso clears his throat. Then he starts reciting:

"We're Big City Scouts.

We're brave and we're true.

We're here to serve others;

that's just what we do.

No matter the problem

we'll solve it ourselves;

we know we can fix it

without any help.

We're here for our families,

our neighbors, our friends.

On the Big City Scouts

you can always depend."

"That was really nice," Tiny says.
"I love poetry."

"It's more than just a poem; it's the
Big City Scouts oath," Grandpa explains.

"It's not in the *Big City Scouts
Handbook*," Velma notes.

"It won't be in that newfangled
handbook, little Street," Grandpa
explains. "The oath is from back in
my day."

"What's an oath?" asks Ralphie.

"An oath is a promise," Grandpa says. "The Big City Scouts oath is what we live by. Got it, Scouts?"

"Got it, sir!" everyone says.

INSTRUCTIONS ARE HELP

So, **what do we** do first?" Louie asks. "I'm ready to start earning badges."

"First we need to put up our tents," Big Lou informs the group. "And by 'we,' I mean you all."

"How do we put them up?" Ralphie asks. "Don't we need instructions?"

"Duh, little Street," says Kurt. "The Big City Scouts oath says we're supposed to solve problems *without any help*."

"Instructions are help," Sid adds.

"We'll also need to unpack the van," Grandpa Ratso says, clapping Big Lou on the shoulder. "That can be your job, sonny boy."

"What are you going to do, Grandpa?" asks Louie.

Grandpa sets up a folding chair. "Why, supervise, of course," he says.

"Now I know where you get it from," Ralphie tells his brother.

The Big City Scouts attempt to put up their tents. It does not go well.

"Why can't I get mine to stay up?" Millicent asks.

"Because you're just a little Street," says Sid. "We had no problem putting *ours* up."

"Except you set yours up on low ground," says Velma. "If you'd read the *Big City Scouts Handbook*, you'd know—"

"You heard Grandpa Ratso. We don't need books," says Kurt.

"Or *nerds* telling us what to do," says Sid.

"I'm not telling you what to do," says Velma. "I'm trying to help."

"We definitely don't need help from little Streets. Us Avenues can do it ourselves," Kurt says.

"Maybe we could 'do it ourselves' together," suggests Millicent. "What do you say, Streets?"

"I'm in," says Velma.

"Me, too," says Tiny. "Mine looks like a wrinkly pancake."

"Speaking of pancakes, where's the food?" Big Lou asks Grandpa Ratso. "I thought you said you were taking care of it."

"I am," says Grandpa Ratso. He picks up two fishing poles and hands one to Big Lou. "Or, shall I say, *we are*. All the food we need is right here, in the great outdoors!"

"Sounds pretty fishy to me," mutters Ralphie. "If you help me with my tent, Louie, I'll share my Happy Puffs with you. Deal?"

"You're on your own, little Street," says Louie. "This Avenue's on his way to earning his Master Camper badge."

"Sounds like a dead end for both of us," Ralphie says. He runs off to join Tiny and Millicent and Velma.

- 3 -

CRACK!

I haven't fished in years. Am I doing it right?" Big Lou wonders.

"You're a Big City Scoutmaster now," Grandpa reminds him. "You shouldn't have to ask."

"What should *we* do?" Ralphie says.

"Why don't you gather some tinder and firewood for the fire," Grandpa says. "We're going to have a lot of fish to fry up soon!"

"Speak for yourself," Big Lou grumbles.

"We're going to forage for greens to make a salad," says Millicent. "Velma knows all the good ones to eat."

"Grandpa's going to double-check them for us, but it's all in the handbook," Velma says.

"There she goes, being nerdy again," Sid says, rolling his eyes.

"Are you guys going to help me gather some firewood?" Ralphie says.

"Duh, we're not supposed to *help*, remember?" Sid says. "You're a Big City Scout—you're supposed to do everything for yourself."

"I'm going to try to earn my Leaf Peeper badge," Louie says. "There are lots of interesting trees around here."

"And Sid and I want to play Frisbee," says Kurt.

Ralphie looks at Tiny. "I guess it's just us Little Streets, then," he says.

"I have a feeling we'll be better off," says Tiny.

When Ralphie and Tiny return, they have armloads of logs for firewood and twigs for tinder.

"I can't wait to sit around the fire and tell stories," says Ralphie. "My dad says that's the best part of camping."

"Do you see something in that tree?" Tiny asks.

"It's not something. It's *someone*," says Ralphie.

"I'm stuck!" cries Louie.

"What's going on?" asks Millicent.

"Our Frisbee got stuck up there, so Louie went after it," Sid explains.

"I thought I could do some good leaf peeping while I was up here," Louie says.

"Now he's too scared to get down," Kurt says.

"I'm n-not s-scared!" Louie insists.

"I'm good at climbing," Tiny says. "I can come up and help you."

"I'll go tell Dad and Grandpa. They'll know what to do," Ralphie says.

"I don't want anyone's help!" cries Louie. "Big City Scouts are supposed to do everything for themselves!"

"Duh, then come down," says Sid.

"Are you crazy?" says Louie. "Have you seen how high up I am?"

"Well, you can't stay up there forever," says Millicent.

"Definitely not," says Velma, assessing the tree. "I see a lot of mushrooms on this trunk, and a lot of dead branches on the ground. From what I've read, those are signs that the tree is damaged or dying."

"When we need your help, we'll ask for it," says Sid. "Which we never will."

CRACK!

The tree branch breaks under Louie's weight.

"Aaaaugh!" he cries, tumbling to the ground.

"Are you OK?" Ralphie asks.

"Yeah, I think so. I landed on something soft," says Louie.

"That's sphagnum moss," Velma notes. "It's also good for insulation or dressing a wound."

"I don't have any *wounds*," Louie insists.

"Except to your pride," Ralphie mutters.

4

MATCHES ARE FOR CHUMPS

When Grandpa Ratso and Big Lou finally return from fishing, Louie groans.

"Finally," he says, rubbing his belly. "I've been working on this tent forever, and I'm hungry."

"Me, too," says Ralphie.

"Well, I hope you're not too hungry," Big Lou says. "We only caught one."

"Just *one* fish? But you were there all afternoon," says Millicent.

"Well, it turns out I'm not much of a fisherman. And Grandpa kept dropping the ones we did catch," Big Lou explains.

"It wasn't my fault," says Grandpa Ratso. "Those fish are just extra slippery."

"I'll cook it up if you make the fire," Big Lou says.

"*You* make the fire," says Grandpa Ratso. "Evidently I'm not as *handy* as you are."

"I know I have matches somewhere," Big Lou says, looking in his pack. Grandpa shakes his head.

"Matches are for chumps. You need to start the fire like a real Big City Scout—all by yourself!" he says.

Big Lou digs a pit and puts rocks around it. He makes sure he has a bucket of water nearby, just in case. Then he tries to start the fire.

"It's not working," whispers Ralphie.

"No worries," says Big Lou. "There are lots of ways to start a fire. That was the Hand Drill Method."

Big Lou tries the Bow Method. Then he tries the Fire Plow. Then he throws up his hands.

"Do you want me to try?" asks Louie.

"Nah, I got this," says Big Lou. But no matter what he does, no fire appears.

"The sticks might not be dry enough," offers Velma. "We could look for new ones. Or we could find the right kind of rock and strike it against a piece of steel."

"We don't have steel," Louie says.

"And it's too dark to look for new sticks or rocks," Ralphie reminds Velma.

"Well, we still have our salad," offers Millicent.

"And we have Happy Puffs," says Ralphie.

"You know, roughing it is actually kind of fun," says Louie.

"Fun? Did you hit your head when you fell out of that tree?" asks Sid.

"Just about everything has gone wrong," Kurt reminds Louie.

"That's just it," says Louie. "We've already had all our bad luck. It's not like things could get any *worse.*"

Just then, it starts to rain.

5

NERD COOTIES

In the morning, the Big City Scouts are very hungry. And Louie and Kurt and Sid are more than a little soggy.

Louie looks at his crumpled tent. "So much for that Master Camper badge," he says. "Why didn't mine stay up like yours?"

"Ours stayed up, but it flooded," Sid says, wringing out his tail.

"We should have set it up on higher ground," Kurt admits. "I hate that Velma was right."

"I told you that you could share my tent with me," says Tiny.

"Avenues don't share tents with little Streets," says Sid.

Kurt sneezes. "Besides, we're all about roughing it," he proclaims.

"I'm all about being *hungry*," says Louie.

"We're all out of Happy Puffs,"
Ralphie says, shaking the empty bag.
"Now what?"

"What are you eating?" Tiny asks
Millicent and Velma.

"Berries," says Millicent. "We just
picked them."

"According to the *Big City Scouts Handbook* and Grandpa Ratso, they're blackberries. Have some," says Velma.

"Thank you *berry* much," says Ralphie, taking a handful.

"It's a beautiful day, Scouts!" says Big Lou. "Who's ready for a hike?"

"We're headed for the Friendly Lookout. It's the most spectacular view in the woods," Grandpa explains.

"Maybe a hike will help my fur dry out," Kurt wonders.

"Maybe I can find more berries," says Louie. "I can earn my Forager badge."

"Do you want to use the handbook?" Velma offers.

"Thanks but no thanks. I think I know what a blackberry looks like, little Street," Louie says.

"Well, Scouts, feast your eyes on the Friendly Lookout," Grandpa Ratso announces.

"Finally," Millicent whispers to Velma. "I thought we'd never get here."

"Whoa," says Sid, taking it all in.

"You weren't kidding about the view, Grandpa," Ralphie says.

"I can see all the way across the woods," says Tiny. "Everything is so . . . green."

"Yeah, green trees, green moss, green little plants with green berries, but not a blackberry bush in sight," says Louie, scratching his paws. "So much for my Forager badge."

"Green little plants with green berries?" says Velma. "Did they have three-leaf clusters?"

"How should I know?" says Louie, still scratching.

"You'd have known if you read the handbook," Velma says. "By the look of that rash on your hands, I think you might have touched some poison ivy."

"Great. Now I'm hungry *and* itchy," says Louie.

"Well, whatever you do, don't scratch it," Velma says. She hands

Louie her canteen. "Here, it will help if you rinse your hands with water."

"No, thanks. I'll treat them myself when we get back to camp," Louie says. He takes off his socks and puts them on his hands. "Maybe I can earn my First Aid badge."

"I've seen this tree before," Millicent says. "Didn't we just pass by it a few minutes ago?"

"Dad, I think we might be lost," Big Lou whispers to Grandpa Ratso.

"Nonsense," says Grandpa. "I know

exactly where we're going. The Friendly Lookout is due south from the campground, so we need to head due north."

"Maybe now would be a good time to consult a map," suggests Big Lou. "Or at least look at a compass?"

"Maps and compasses are for chumps. I know these trails like the back of my hand," says Grandpa. "Everyone follow me!"

"We'd better be on the right track," Louie says. "I'm itching to get back to camp."

When Big Lou isn't looking, Ralphie

grabs his phone.

"What are you doing?" asks Louie.

"I think it's time we got some help," Ralphie explains.

"But we're Big City Scouts," Louie reminds him. "We're not supposed to ask for—"

"Would you rather lose your Scout cred, or keep being hungry, tired, lost . . . and *itchy*?" Ralphie says.

"You have a point," says Louie. "Can you find a map with some trails?"

Ralphie searches and searches.

"Nope," he says. Then he gets an idea. "But this phone will help us find something better: reinforcements."

The Big City Scouts keep walking. And walking. And walking.

"Are we lost?" asks Tiny. "I think we're lost."

"It feels like we've been out here *forever*," Ralphie says, checking his watch.

"I'm tired," says Kurt.

"I'm itchy, and now my hands smell like my feet," says Louie, rubbing at his socks.

"I'm starving," says Sid. "We should have eaten some of Velma's berries."

"You said they had nerd cooties," Kurt reminds him.

"Aren't there other ways to figure out where we are?" asks Ralphie. "Like, doesn't moss grow on the north sides of trees or something?"

"That's a myth," Velma informs him. "Moss grows on wet surfaces with no sun. The north side is the one that gets less sun during the day, so if you find a vertical object with moss on one side, that's probably the north."

"But these trees have moss everywhere," notes Millicent. "They must not get much sun at all."

"No worries. I have an idea," says Velma, consulting her handbook. "Ralphie, can I see your watch?"

"Sure," says Ralphie.

"We point the hour hand to the sun, then we draw an imaginary line halfway between that and the twelve. That direction is south, so the opposite is north," says Velma. "Grandpa said that the campground is due north, so if we go in that direction, we're sure to find our way back."

"Whoa," says Sid.

"I'm starting to think I might *want* nerd cooties," says Kurt.

"Duh," says Velma.

"Nice work," Big Lou tells her.

"I would have gotten us back to the campsite sooner or later," Grandpa Ratso insists.

"Dad," says Big Lou, "even the best of us need a hand sometimes."

"Not me. Not ever," says Grandpa Ratso.

"Well, I think asking for help is just as admirable as offering it," says Big Lou. "I remember a certain young rat coming to his dad for help when he wanted to ask out a girl he liked."

"Was that girl Mama?" Louie asks. Mama Ratso isn't with them anymore, but she's always in their hearts. Just thinking about her takes Louie's mind off his poison ivy.

"That's right," says Big Lou. "I knew she liked birds, so I asked Grandpa to teach me all about them. Without his help, I don't think Mama would have said yes to me."

"And you might not have ended up marrying her," notes Grandpa.

"And then we wouldn't be here!" Ralphie adds.

Big Lou nods. "Maybe it's time you admit you need a hand sometimes, too," he says.

Grandpa sighs.

"You might be right," he says. "I'm starting to see things more clearly now. Well, not literally. Now that it's getting dark, did anyone bring flashlights?"

"Game ON!" say Louie and Ralphie.

"Let's go, Ratsos," says Big Lou, leading the way.

6

HELLO, FELLAS!

When the Big City Scouts finally find their way back, they see a green truck parked next to Grandpa's red one.

"Wait," says Big Lou. "That looks familiar."

"Grandma!" shout Louie and Ralphie.

"Hello, fellas!" says Grandma Ratso. "How are my Big City Scouts doing?"

"We've . . . been better," Big Lou admits. "What are you doing here?"

"A little bird told me you might need some help," she says. She gives Louie and Ralphie a wink. "Well, maybe *two* little birds."

"I admit it: I do need help," Grandpa says. "Even if that means I'm in violation of the Big City Scouts oath." He clears his throat.

"We're Big City Scouts.

We're brave and we're true.

We're here to serve others;

that's just what we do.

No matter the problem

we'll solve it ourselves;

we know we can fix it

without any help.

We're here for our families,

our neighbors, our friends.

On the Big City Scouts

you can always depend."

"You're saying the most important line wrong, dear," says Grandma Ratso.

"No matter the problem

we'll solve it ourselves;

and if we can't fix it

we'll reach out for help."

"What a relief!" says Grandpa.

"Now, that makes more sense," says Louie.

"I was a Big City Scout, too, back in the day," Grandma Ratso says. "In fact, Grandpa Ratso and I met on a camping trip just like this. I showed him how to bait his fishing hook."

"Even the best of us needs a hand sometimes," Grandpa says, giving Big Lou a wink.

"Thanks for coming, Grandma," Ralphie whispers.

"I'm proud of you boys for calling me," she says. "It's important to admit when you're in trouble. Good thing I brought reinforcements."

Grandma pulls a cooler out of the back of her truck. She opens it.

"FOOD!" everyone shouts.

"And calamine lotion," Louie says, sighing.

"And matches. Thank goodness,"
says Big Lou.

"It's a little damp out here for
starting a fire the old-fashioned way,"
Grandma notes. "Now, who wants to

help make Grandma Ratso's Famous Campfire Chili?"

"Me-me-me-me-me!" everyone shouts, Grandpa Ratso loudest of all.

"I thought you were all about roughing it," Grandma Ratso says.

"I'm all about your chili," says Grandpa. "Roughing it is for chumps."

7

S'MORE HELP

And that's how I caught the biggest fish on my very first Big City Scouts camping trip," says Grandpa.

"I think you just had the right bait on your hook," says Grandma. "Thanks to yours truly."

"You might be right. Though I did reel in another good catch on that trip, all by myself," Grandpa says, giving her a squeeze.

"Good stories and good food by the fire," says Ralphie. "The scouting life is sweet."

"This tastes a lot like *your* chili, Dad," says Louie.

"Where do you think he got the recipe?" says Grandma Ratso.

"Grandma is a wise woman," says Grandpa Ratso. "She knows just about everything."

"And when I don't know something, I'm glad you're around to help me," she says, giving him a nudge.

"I think we've all learned something on this trip," Big Lou says. "In fact, I think you're all going to earn Master Camper badges. Louie and Ralphie will be earning Emergency badges, for taking initiative when we were in trouble. Velma and Millicent will earn Forager badges, for making sure we had plenty of healthy berries and salad. And Velma will also earn an

Ingenuity badge, for finding a way out of the woods today."

"Wow," says Velma, taking out her calculator. "Now I have almost a dozen!"

"I knew you had potential!" says Millicent.

"Velma has more badges than we have," Kurt says to Sid.

"Way more," says Sid. "Maybe we should get some calculators."

"And do some reading," adds Kurt.

"With two new badges, my Scout vest is going to look even cooler," says Louie.

"I'll help you iron them on, since you probably won't be able to use your hands for a while," says Ralphie.

"Thanks, brother," says Louie. "You've taught me a lot on this trip."

"*I've* taught *you*?" says Ralphie.

"Yep," says Louie. "You might think you're just a little Street, but you're really going places."

"Since being a Big City Scout is all about helping," says Tiny, "I'll have a second *helping* of chili!"

"Life is much easier when we admit we can't do everything ourselves," says Big Lou.

"And when we help each other!" says Millicent, putting her arm around Velma.

"Duh, I won't need any help eating all these s'mores by myself," says Sid.

"Well, we're all going to try," says Louie.

"The scouting life *is* sweet!" says Ralphie.